The Pantomime Witch

Written by
Hannah Cole

Illustrated by
D. S. Aldridge

IDEALS CHILDREN'S BOOKS
Nashville, Tennessee

There was going to be a children's show at the theater. It was called *Hansel and Gretel*, and everyone could see from the posters that there was a witch in it.

Carole knew all about the theater, because she had been to see *Puss in Boots* last year. But Angela had never seen a show, so Carole told her all about it.

"There are hundreds of seats in straight lines," she said. "And you have to sit in the one with your number on it. You have to sit very still and not kick the people in front of you. Then the lights go out, and the music begins, and you see the story happening on the stage. It isn't real, of course. It's only grown-ups pretending to be the people in the story."

For Jacob, Dora and Conrad
H.C.

For my dearest friend, Peter M. Cronin
D.A.

First published in the United States by
Ideals Publishing Corporation
Nelson Place at Elm Hill Pike
Nashville, Tennessee 37214

First published in Great Britain by
Julia MacRae Books
A division of Walker Books, Ltd.
London, England

Printed in Hong Kong

Library of Congress Cataloging-in-Publication Data

Cole, Hannah, 1954
    The pantomime witch.

    Summary: An adventure begins when Grandpa takes
his two granddaughters to the theater to see a production
of "Hansel and Gretel" and one of the girls drops her
teddy bear off the balcony.
    (1. Theater – Fiction. 2. Grandfathers – Fiction.
3. Teddy bears – Fiction. I. Aldridge, D.S.,
1956   , ill. II. Title.
PZ7.C673439Pan 1990   [E]   90-4385

ISBN 0-8249-8462-5

"Will the witch be real?" Angela asked. "With a broomstick?"

"Well, she will have a broomstick," said Carole. "But it will only be an ordinary person dressed up as a witch."

"But she will do real magic, won't she?" asked Angela.

"Oh, yes," said Carole. "Of course, she will do real magic."

Carole and Angela's grandpa bought three tickets for the show. He invited Carole and Angela to go to the theater with him.

"May I see the tickets?" asked Angela. They were just three little scraps of paper with writing printed on them.

"These are good seats," said Grandpa. "They are in Row A, right at the very front of the upstairs balcony, so I think we will have about the best view in the whole theater."

2

Carole and Angela had to put on their best dresses to go to the theater and have their hair brushed very hard. Angela didn't like her best dress.

"You look lovely," said Grandpa. "Everyone will think that you're the most beautiful child in the theater."

"Row A isn't too close to the stage, is it?" Angela asked.

"Oh, it's close enough," said Grandpa. "You will be able to see everything perfectly."

"But will everything be able to see me?" asked Angela. "What about the witch?"

"No, no," said Grandpa. "The witch will never notice you among the hundreds and hundreds of other children."

Angela messed up her hair just in case, so that she wouldn't show up too well by being the most beautiful child in the theater.

Angela wanted to take her teddy bear, Fergus, with her to the theater.

"Oh, no!" groaned Carole. "Not Fergus! Grandpa, she can't take that old bear to the theater! I'm not going with her if she takes it. Tell her she can't."

"Well, I don't see that it will do any harm if she does take it," said Grandpa. "It's such a little thing. It can't get in anyone's way."

So Fergus was allowed to go. If he hadn't been allowed to go, Angela wouldn't have gone. She put him in his best clothes.

The balcony was upstairs in the theater. The stairs had purple carpet on them and golden handrails at the side.

"You don't have to jump up every step," said Carole. "You're supposed to walk properly in a theater."

But they were such wide steps, with such soft carpet on them, that it was hard to walk properly. Angela jumped and Fergus slid up the handrail. Grandpa didn't mind.

They found Row A and walked along until they came to their seats. Angela's seat was a very good one — red and furry. There was a shelf in front of it; but if Angela sat on the edge of her seat and leaned forward, she could see the whole theater. There were huge curtains hiding the stage and large pillars on either side. Down below, on the floor of the theater, there were rows and rows of seats. From up in Row A of the balcony, Angela could see right down on top of the heads of the people sitting there.

"These are very good seats, aren't they, Grandpa?" asked Carole.

"Wonderful," said Grandpa. "We couldn't have a better view. Sit down, Angela, and don't lean over or I will have to hold on to you." He had brought a bag of candy and they each had a piece while they waited for the show to start.

3

At last the lights began to grow dim, and there was a sound of drums. Angela sat up very straight and held Fergus up on the shelf in front of her so that he could watch the curtains opening.

"Remember, you have to be very quiet," whispered Carole to Angela.

"I am," Angela whispered back.

"And don't fidget," whispered Carole.

"I'm not," said Angela.

"Can't you put that silly bear away?" said Carole.

"No," whispered Angela.

The show began. Hansel and Gretel were very poor. They lived in a cottage in the woods and they hardly had anything to eat. Angela already knew the story and she felt very sorry for the two children on the stage. Every now and then she picked up Fergus and whispered into his ear to explain the story. Then she put him back on the shelf.

When the witch flew onto the stage, everyone gasped. She was green all over — even her hair — and she looked terrible. She kept pointing at people with her bony, green finger. Angela hoped that

she wouldn't point at her or Fergus. She held Fergus tightly and covered his eyes so that he wouldn't be frightened.

"Don't be scared," whispered Grandpa. "Here, have another piece of candy."

Angela put Fergus down on the shelf for a minute while she unwrapped the candy.

Suddenly Carole groaned. Angela looked at her in surprise. Carole was hiding her face in her hands.

"What's wrong with you?" Grandpa asked. "Too much candy already?"

Carole looked up. Her face was bright red. "I told you not to let Angela bring that stupid bear!" she moaned. "She brought it and now she's dropped it over the edge. Oh, Grandpa, take Angela home. She's embarrassing me!"

Angela looked around in horror. Sure enough, Fergus was missing. He must have fallen right over the front of the balcony. Angela leaned over the shelf and looked down to the rows of seats below. The people down below were not watching the witch on the stage. They were all looking up to see where the flying bear had come from. But the whole theater was dark, with only a faint green light coming from the witch's cauldron, and Angela could not see Fergus at all.

Then the people downstairs stopped looking up and turned back to the stage so they wouldn't miss the show.

"Sit down!" hissed someone behind Angela. "We can't see if you stand up."

Grandpa pulled Angela back into her seat. "Don't worry," he whispered. "We'll find your teddy bear after the show. Just sit back and enjoy yourself."

But Angela could not enjoy herself with Fergus missing. Suppose someone downstairs liked him and decided to keep Fergus?

Then Angela would never see him again. Thinking about that made her cry.

"Tell her to stop sniffing," whispered Carole. "You're not supposed to sniff at the theater."

Grandpa felt sorry for Angela. "It's all right," he whispered. "I'll go downstairs and find your teddy bear right away. You wave your hand when you see me, and then I'll know where you dropped it."

He got up and squeezed along to the end of the row, then disappeared down the stairs.

The witch was still being horrible on the stage.

4

Angela peeped over the edge of the shelf. At last she saw Grandpa far below, looking lost in the darkness. She waved to him, and he waved back as he set off along the row of seats just below them. Now Angela knew that he would find Fergus, and that everything would be all right. She began to watch the witch again.

"Ha ha!" the witch was cackling. "I feel like a bit of magic! Now what shall I do? Shall I turn you all into spiders?" she shouted, pointing at all the children watching the show.

"No!" the audience screamed.

"Shall I turn you all into toads?"

"No!"

The witch shook her nasty fingers, and Angela could hear her fingernails clicking.

"I shall have to turn somebody into something," said the witch, "or I shall explode." Suddenly she pointed at someone downstairs. "You, sir! I shall turn you into something! Come up here on the stage, if you please!"

"I wonder who it is," whispered Carole. "Do you think she will really turn him into something?"

"I think she will," said Angela. "I hope it's somebody horrible, who deserves it."

But when the person got up on the stage with the witch and the green lights were shining on him, they could see who it was. It was not anyone horrible. It was Grandpa and he was holding Fergus.

"Look," said Carole. "He did find your silly bear."

"But the witch is going to turn him into a toad!" cried Angela. "Tell her to stop!"

"Stop talking," whispered Carole. "You aren't supposed to talk at the theater."

Grandpa did not look frightened at all. He was laughing.

"Step into my cauldron, if you please," said the witch, and she picked up Grandpa's leg and put it into the cauldron.

"Ouch," said Grandpa. "It's boiling." Everyone could hear what he said quite clearly, because he was near the microphones on the stage.

"Now the other leg," said the witch. "Both feet in, double quick."

But the cauldron was too small for Grandpa to put both his feet in.

"You're too big," said the witch. "Too big and too fat. I need someone smaller to work my wicked magic on." She looked around.

"Do you think she will let Grandpa go now?" whispered Angela.

"She might," said Carole.

Then the witch noticed Fergus in Grandpa's hand.

"Aha!" she hissed. "I see you have a cat with you. You must be a witch like me. Give me that cat and I shall turn it into a toad."

"He isn't a cat!" Angela shouted as loud as she could. "He's a bear, and you better not turn him into anything, you horrible pig witch!"

"Ssh," said Carole. "You aren't supposed to be rude to the actors."

But with the cauldron crackling and the band playing scary music, the witch did not hear Angela anyway. She snatched Fergus from Grandpa's hand and made some magic signs over him. Then she scattered some magic dust around him and walked in a circle.

5

Suddenly, in the witch's hand, there wasn't a bear any more, just a big, green toad which hopped off her hand and vanished into the cauldron. This was the worst thing that had ever happened in Angela's whole life. It was too terrible even to make her cry. Grandpa was looking quite horrified as well.

"I think you had better turn it back again, if you don't mind," he said to the witch. "That teddy bear belonged to my granddaughter, and she was very fond of it."

"I don't know about that," said the witch. "The magic may not work twice. We'll see. I shall need a little help. Will you help me?" she called out to everyone who was watching the show.

"Yes!" they all screamed back. Angela screamed the loudest of all.

"When I sprinkle the magic dust into the cauldron," said the witch, "you must say the magic spell as loud as you can. Split, splat, come back, cat!"

She sprinkled the magic dust, and everyone in the theater shouted as loud as they could, "Split, splat, come back, cat!"

Angela screamed, "Split, splat, come back, Fergus!"

The witch reached her bony, green arm into the cauldron. Angela held her breath.

Grandpa was peering into the cauldron and looking rather nervous.

"Suppose she has turned him into a cat?" said Angela. "I don't want a cat."

But it was all right. The witch pulled Fergus out of the cauldron, and Grandpa snatched him back from her.

"Thank you," said Grandpa, and he hurried off the stage.

The witch just carried on with her wicked spells while Angela waited for Grandpa to get back upstairs.

At last he arrived, out of breath from running up all the steps. He gave Fergus to Angela.

"Oh, thank you, Grandpa," said Angela. "You were wonderful."

"Don't drop it again," said Grandpa. "I didn't expect to have to rescue it from a witch."

Angela kept Fergus on her lap after that and held him very tightly. He looked okay. You would never have guessed that he had just been turned into a toad.

At last the show ended. Hansel and Gretel tricked the witch and turned her into gingerbread. Everyone clapped and cheered. Angela couldn't clap, because she did not dare let go of Fergus; but she cheered and cheered until Carole said, "You aren't really supposed to scream your head off at the theater."

Fergus was sparkling with the magic dust that the witch had sprinkled over him. It stayed in his fur for weeks. Carole said it was only glitter, but anyone could see that it was magic.